Cup of Secrets

Trace of Lace

Finding Home Mystery Short Stories

Barbara Howard

This is a work of fiction. Similarities to real people, places, or events are entirely coincidental.

CUP OF SECRETS - TRACE OF LACE

First edition. March 1, 2022.

Copyright © 2022 Barbara Howard.

ISBN: 979-8201346195

Written by Barbara Howard.

Table of Contents

CUP OF SECRETS

"The idea of mixing birthday balloons and Christmas decorations in one party theme sounded crazy to me," Jules said as she walked through the Parkers' entrance hall. "I guess that's what happens when you're born on Christmas Day. You know what? It looks pretty nice." She spun around. "I really like it. No, I love it!"

"Me, too." Milo surveyed the main foyer, then stepped inside the grand room and scanned the space from the glossy maple wood dance floor to the rustic vaulted ceiling. Everything looked perfect. "You did an awesome job, babe. I'm so proud of you."

"We did it." She slipped her arms around his waist and gave him a kiss on the cheek.

"What are you doing?" Milo blushed and glanced around.

"It's mistletoe," Jules said, wiping her lipstick stain from his face. She pointed to the little sprig of greenery hanging above their heads.

"Well, Merry Mistletoe." He smiled and watched as Jules sauntered off to the kitchen, glancing back at him with the sweetest grin. He took a deep breath and studied the event checklist for the millionth time.

The last year had been a grind, with very little money and even less sleep. The hard work had paid off when he landed the most sought-after holiday party in the county. The budget was through the roof, no limits. This one event would cover his operating expenses through the next quarter and prove to Mr. Latimore that he was worthy of Jules. Her parents were still skeptical, and their relationship had suffered from it. He could provide a good future for her with this catering business. It would just take time. Working for the Parkers had put him on the map with a whole new affluent clientele. No more backyard barbecues and swim parties. Requests were already coming in and the evening had not started yet. He stared at the list, double-checking every detail, and totally missed Chelsea Parker's presence next to him.

"So, here's my birthday present," she said and slipped her arms around his shoulders, then traced her fingers up and down his arms, smiling mischievously at him.

"Oh, wow." Milo blinked and took a quick breath. "I didn't see you come in. Happy birthday, Chelsea. It's going to be the best party you've ever had."

"You promise?" She licked her lips and tightened her grip. Her golden blonde hair was pulled into a high ponytail. She wore twinkling candy cane earrings and a hunter green bodysuit. If Naughty Santa's Elf was the look she was going for, she had nailed it.

"He is not your present, Chelsea." Jules walked over and pried her fingers away. "I think you should touch up your makeup, by the way."

Chelsea patted her face where her mascara had run in jagged lines down her cheeks and smiled. "I suppose you're right. Thanks, hun." She looked Milo up and down, then walked down the hall to the master suite.

Milo turned to Jules and shrugged. He hoped the two women would avoid each other during the party as much as possible.

"I really don't like her, you know. She thinks she can have everything and everyone." Jules folded her arms and watched Chelsea close the bedroom door. "Don't worry. I won't say anything to her right now. But she'll learn to keep her hands off you after tonight. I hate ..."

"Forget about it." Milo couldn't let the tension escalate between those two. He put his hands on her waist and lowered his head to make direct eye contact. "She's probably drunk. Besides, after tonight I think you and me need to talk about us, being permanent. You know? Forever. And I don't mean just the business partnership." Mr. Latimore needed to get over it. Jules was the center of his life, and nothing was going to stop them from being together. He stroked his fingertips along her cheek. Jules gave him a little grin, and then that radiant smile was back.

"What about grad school next year?" she said softly and wrinkled her brow. "My parents ..."

Milo brushed his lips against her earlobe and whispered, "We'll talk about it later, okay?"

"So, you two are making out when you should be working. Good thing I came to check on you." Traci Simmons rushed into the room like a hurricane, which was her usual style.

"We're working, trust me," Milo said, and gave her a hug. He could always depend on Traci to step into a situation to make sure everything was in order and up to her standards. It was annoying, but he loved that about her. She slipped off the navy barn coat with the burgundy Hazelton House crest embroidered on the pockets and draped it across the nearest armchair. She must have come directly from volunteering for the annual Christmas concert and sleigh rides at Bent Willow Farm.

"Jules, here's the seating chart." Traci pulled out the instructions from her overflowing pockets. "Go ahead and get the place cards on the table. I'll help BAMJoe get set up to deejay in the other room. And here's the floor plan of the house for you, too. This place has way too many rooms, in my opinion. Try not to open the wrong door, like I did. Randall is home alone with little Remy. I promised I wouldn't stay long. Everything alright, Milo?" He nodded as she scurried out of sight. Milo took another deep breath and thought, "Yes, everything is perfect."

BAMJoe got the music started, and the guests crowded into the center of the grand room to dance. Chelsea had reappeared and was standing in front of the pink flocked Christmas tree pretending to hang ornaments as her friends snapped pictures and shared them online. Mr. and Mrs. Parker stood in the corner of the room with arms folded, not smiling. Very odd. They both wore beige like camouflage. John Parker in plaid cardigan and slacks, and his wife Shanice in a body hugging floor-length knit. Mr. Parker glanced at his watch and looked around the room. Milo avoided eye contact with them and headed to the kitchen. It was almost time to start dinner service. Before he could get out of sight, Chelsea started shouting. She was locked arm in arm with Carlton Burnhart.

"Listen up, everybody," Chelsea clapped her hands and waved for BAMJoe to stop the music. Everyone groaned and turned to face her. "I've got an announcement to make," she shouted as Carlton tried to cover her mouth and they wrestled playfully.

"C'mon! Tell us!" The crowd grew restless in anticipation.

"Go ahead and announce your engagement and make your parents happy!" John Parker yelled from across the room. There was a collective gasp from the crowd, then cheers and laughter.

"Oh, no!" Chelsea said and turned around, motioning to the crowd to follow her outside. "Everybody let's get pictures by the bonfire. Then it'll be time to eat next. Hurry up!"

Within seconds, the entire room emptied into the side yard and Milo was left standing alone. "That was weird," he mumbled and looked out of the bay window at the group huddled together, laughing and teasing each other while Sergio, the videographer, tried to do his job. No one followed his directions. Chelsea led the crowd in singing a mashup of Christmas carols and Carlton bellowed out showtunes at the same time. What a mess.

"So, she was coming onto me just a few minutes ago, but she has a boyfriend. Or fiancée?"

Whatever was going on between Chelsea and Carlton, Milo didn't want involved. He picked up a torch from a service cart and lit the candelabras in the center of each table that were arranged in a circle around the perimeter of the room. The place settings were glistening. It was a beautiful space. He took out his phone and snapped a few quick photos. Chelsea and Mrs. Parker had tasted and approved each dish on the menu. For the first time in weeks, a wave of relief swept over him. He stepped into the kitchen and helped Jules plate the first course. Her hands moved swiftly and gracefully over the dishes, adding garnish, and adjusting portions. He could watch her all night. So beautiful. She wore a black apron with a matching cap over a neat bun, small gold dangle earrings (his Christmas gift to her) and the candy apple red lipstick that he loved.

"Big checks coming our way after this." He smiled and wiped the rims of each plate. "We just have to make it through the night."

"We got this," Jules said and patted his shoulder. "No worries."

• • • •

MILO RUBBED THE BACK of his neck and stretched, then sat down at the little desk in the corner of his kitchen. He had been too exhausted after Chelsea's party last night to do anything except collapse on the sofa and try to get a few hours of sleep. Jules called and offered to come over with coffee, chocolate croissants, and bagels. They would go over the paperwork for the Parkers, inventory the supplies, and finish cleaning all the service ware. While he waited for Jules, Milo scrolled through his phone and jotted down the fresh contacts he had made from the party. New business from at least four people with more on the way. A bachelor party, retirement luncheon, anniversary, and baby shower at the N.D. Lewis Country Club. He needed to work on estimates and sample platters for each one. His head was spinning, but this was his dream for his life with Jules by his side. It was their time. He could feel it.

"Hello beautiful," he said and held back a yawn as Jules walked in the back door. "And Merry Christmas!"

"Milo, did you get my text?"

"No, I think my notifications are still off from last night. Why? What's up?" He rose, kissed her cheek, grabbed a coffee, then searched the bag and scored the only asiago cheese bagel.

"Check your phone." Jules sat down and stared at him.

"Why? Just tell me." He sliced the bagel in half and smeared it with his favorite butter from Dawson's local creamery. "Mmm, so good. Y'know, old man Dawson could charge me a hundred bucks a pound for this stuff, and I'd still buy it."

"Milo."

He put down the bagel and sat next to her. There was something in her tone that made him uneasy. And he couldn't identify her expression. What was it? Worry. Fear. Sleep deprived, for sure. "What's going on, babe?"

"Chelsea. She's dead."

"No, you're wrong. That's not ... Okay, wait." He stood and studied her face again. Was this some kind of mean joke? He tried to respond, but his mind kept racing back through images from the previous night, just a few short hours ago. "That can't be true. Where'd you get that from? Who told you that?"

"It's all over. Everybody's talking about it."

"When? What happened?"

"I don't know. I don't know."

Milo paced around the little table and looked at his phone. There were dozens of text messages waiting. He started to open the first one and froze as Traci burst through the back door with little Remy on her hip. The toddler was barely awake in his reindeer print pajamas. He held a juice pouch in his fist and rested his face under Traci's chin.

"Did you hear about Chelsea Parker? Can you believe it? I asked Randall to find out whatever he can. Even though he's not on the police force anymore, he still has connections, you know." She gripped Milo by the shoulder, searching for a response. He had none.

"I'll get that," Jules said and gently brushed her hand across his back on her way to answer the knock at the front door that only she had noticed.

Milo pulled out his phone again. His first impulse was to contact the Parkers. Or maybe that wasn't the best idea. He stared at the news alert that popped up on his phone. Chelsea's high school graduation photo was under the headline, Investigation Underway After Chelsea Parker of Layne

Township Found Dead. "Today's her birthday. She was only eighteen. I don't believe it."

"Believe it," Randall said as he appeared at the back door and came inside to join them. "And don't answer the door."

"Why?" Milo asked, but it was too late.

Jules walked into the room with two KMP officers following her. "Milo, they need to talk to you."

"Me?"

"Hey Gonz, what's going on?" Randall stepped across the room and shook hands with one of the men.

"Hey Randall, it's been a while. This doesn't involve you, so …"

"Oh, I think it does." Randall folded his arms across his chest and widened his stance. "Everything around here involves me."

"And me," Traci said and stood beside her husband.

"Alright." The officer turned to Milo. "I'm Detective Gonzales. This is Officer Edmonds. You probably have already heard about the Parkers' daughter, Chelsea. I'll be leading the investigation into the incident. Mrs. Shanice Parker said that you catered a party at their home last night and might have some information regarding Chelsea's death."

"Me? How? I just brought the food. I mean, I didn't have anything to do with Chelsea last night. Or anybody, really. I just handled the food, you know. It's what I do."

Detective Gonzales stepped closer to Milo. "Mrs. Parker stated that you prepared a dish specifically for her daughter and no one else. Is that correct?"

Milo wiped his sweating palms on a napkin and cleared his throat. "Yeah, that's right. Chelsea told me the flavors that she liked, so I came up with something. I figured if she liked it, then

I would add it to the menu for my next gig. I already had a few people hit me up at the party, so..."

"So, it's true that no one else ate any of it?"

Randall directed Traci to step aside as he crossed between Milo and the detective. "Hold it. Don't answer that, son." He turned back to face Gonzales. "Why are you here?"

"We need to gather the menu, recipes, ingredients, and all kitchen items that were used for the event last night. The autopsy report will reveal the cause of death, but in the meantime, we have to log everything. You understand, Randall."

Milo searched Randall's face. "Wait. Is he saying that I ... Randall, what does he mean?"

Randall glanced back at him. "Milo, keep your mouth shut."

Gonzales looked at Randall and unveiled a slight grin. "We have a warrant."

Randall lifted his chin. "Is it signed?"

"Judge Hurdock."

Randall took the document from him, checked the signature, scanned the details, then handed it back to him. "Okay, Milo. Take him through, but only give him what is on that list and nothing else. And don't say anything. You got that?"

"Yeah." Milo nodded and glanced at Jules, who was standing in the corner, her eyes welling over with tears. He led the two men into the small room attached to the kitchen that he used as a prep and staging area. "I'll get the menu for the party. And the ingredients."

"And the special item that you made."

"Oh yeah, that's not written down anywhere. Basically, it's egg whites. A meringue is what it's called. Almond flavoring. The good kind, not the imitation, with coconut folded in. I used pink food coloring because that's Chelsea's favorite color. Was. Was her favorite color. Anyway, I put the recipe on a note card in the file. Pink Kisses is what I named it."

"Kisses?" Jules spoke up and wiped her tears. "Really, Milo?"

"It's just a name, Jules. I didn't know Chelsea like that."

Randall cleared his throat softly and narrowed his eyes at Milo. "Steady, steady."

Milo nodded at Randall and lowered his voice. "I can't help that it's easier for me." He turned toward Officer Gonzales and whispered, "I don't know how to spell meringue." He shrugged and handed him the note card with the recipe.

Jules stepped toward the pantry door. "Come with me, please. I can help you find everything you need." Milo tried to make eye contact with her as she escorted the men to the main supply area, but she refused to look at him.

Randall tapped Milo on the arm. "Stand here with me. And stop talking. Got that?"

Milo nodded and stared at the floor. How could he have the perfect night and wake up to a nightmare like this? If they took all of his tools and supplies, how would he keep working? What if people found out?

"They're taking everything," he whispered. "What am I going to tell everybody when I can't show up?"

"Nothing." Randall said. His tone was cold and his face as expressionless as a stone. Milo swallowed his words and wiped his forehead.

Finally, the men exited the pantry with two cardboard boxes and three large trash bags full of "evidence" and thanked them for their cooperation. The detective smiled gently at Jules that made Milo uncomfortable. He stepped forward, but Randall pulled him back.

"Juliana Latimore, right? There's video footage from a security camera at the Parkers' home," Gonzales said, still smiling. "It shows that you returned to the property last night, after the party."

"Hold up before you say anything, Jules. Video quality can be unreliable. You know that, Gonz." Randall's impatience was radiating through the room. Everyone was tense. Even little Remy was fidgeting in his mother's arms.

"Sure," Gonzales said without lifting his gaze from Jules. "Did you?"

"Umm, that's right. I did."

Randall let out a sigh and threw up his hands in frustration.

"Can you tell me what you were doing there?" Gonzales said, ignoring everyone else in the room. His eyes fixed on Jules, the smile unwavering.

"I came back to get something that I forgot when we cleaned up."

"What was that?"

"One of our large banquet trays. I forgot to pack it up with the rest of the supplies. We had to special order it, so I didn't want to ..."

Randall cleared his throat and shook his head at her.

"Anyway, I just went in the side patio entrance near the kitchen and got it. That's all."

"Was anyone else in the kitchen when you entered?"

"No. No one else was there."

Traci pushed Jules aside and stood in front of the detective. "I don't know why you're questioning her when you should be talking to the boyfriend. What's his name? Carson?

"Carlton." Milo and Jules said in unison.

"Okay, yeah. Carlton. Chelsea got in a fight with him in the bedroom. I saw it. She was pretty mad."

"You were there? Why?" Randall gripped his forehead and pursed his lips.

"A fight?" Gonzales asked.

"Well, an argument," Traci continued. "She was going to throw him out, but he begged her and started crying. So, she gave in and ..."

"What were they arguing about?"

"I couldn't hear everything. But what I could tell ..."

"Again. Why were you there?" Randall raised his voice.

Traci looked at Randall and softened her voice. "It was a big night for Milo. I wanted to be there to make sure everything went okay. You know how I am."

"Exactly." Randall looked at the ceiling and took a deep breath. He shook his head and looked at her face, almost pleading. "I do. That's why I want you to stop talking and stay out of this."

"What did you say the boyfriend's name is?" Gonzales asked, undeterred.

"Carlos," Traci said quickly, before Randall could object.

"Carlton," Jules responded. "Carlton Burnhart."

"Thank you. I'll speak with Mr. and Mrs. Parker about this." Gonzales smiled at Jules again, but she turned away and stood beside Milo.

"I'll walk you out." Randall motioned toward the front door and the two officers stepped out of the room ahead of him. The others remained in the kitchen.

"Jules, what you said just then," Milo whispered and turned to face her, his brow wrinkled with concern. "You lied."

"What are you talking about?" She averted her gaze.

"About leaving the tray. Why did you sneak back into their house? Did you go back to see Chelsea? Were you still mad about me and her? I mean, you said that she would learn her lesson. Or something like that."

"Do you think that I would kill someone over you?"

"I don't know why you ..." Milo paused. His memory flipped through the images of Chelsea and the jealous looks from Jules. "Why you would lie to me about something like this? That's all."

"I didn't lie. I just didn't tell you."

"Why not?"

"Milo, I just ..." Jules turned away and started crying.

Traci walked over and touched her cheek. "It doesn't matter right now. Let's deal with what we know for sure. Okay? What did Detective Gonzales say to you?"

"I asked him what happened to Chelsea. He couldn't tell me but said they would find out soon."

"Who would want to kill her?" Milo said, lost in thought.

"Anybody. Everybody," Jules said, wiping away her tears and regaining her composure.

"What? She's pretty popular. Or was." Milo looked up in disbelief.

"Money can buy you lots of company, but not real friends. Nobody liked Chelsea. Not just me, Milo." She glared at him.

"It's a well-known secret that she couldn't wait to leave Keeferton because her parents ..."

"I'm not saying you had anything to do with what happened. We don't even know what happened. You can't believe everything you hear around town." His nervousness gave way to anger. "And, by the way, a well-known secret is not a secret."

"Never mind." Jules turned away and walked to the opposite side of the kitchen.

"What did I say?" Milo looked at Traci, expecting cover. "It's true, right?"

"So, Gonzales has video evidence and probably confiscated everything from Sergio, too. What do we have?" Traci carried on.

"I have a few pictures that I took with my phone. Mainly the dining area. That's all I was concerned about." Milo opened his phone and found the album containing the pictures.

Traci scrolled through them and paused. "Something's not right about this one."

"Hmm," Milo enlarged the picture of Chelsea seated for dinner. "Where's Carlton?"

"Exactly!" Traci said and zoomed in to make the picture even larger. "That's not the original seating plan. Those place cards are all in the wrong order. Who is that next to Chelsea?"

"Jules. What happened?"

"What?" Jules peeked at the picture and stepped back. "I did my best with those cards, but the lighting was so dim in the room. Maybe I mixed them up. I don't know." She waved her arms. "I'm not used to reading by candlelight, Milo. What did you expect?" She stormed out of the room. Traci looked up at Milo, shrugged and gave him back the phone.

"Settle down, everybody," Randall said as he rejoined them, with Jules in tow. "Here's what I know, so far. The Parkers have ordered a private autopsy and are demanding all additional reports be expedited. Normally it takes weeks, but they want answers before New Year's."

"That's impossible!" Traci said. "I can't blame them for trying, though."

"Judge Hurdock is Shanice Parker's uncle. And, you know what they say, money talks. I expect things to get done fast, and more than a few rules broken along the way.

"I can't imagine what it's like. Chelsea was their only child. Do they think it was an accident, or ..." Traci held her son tightly against her chest.

"In good health. No known drug use. They found her body on the kitchen floor. So yeah, they suspect someone had a hand in this. Unless there was a reason that she would take her own life. Who knows?"

"That detective, he knows. He scares me," Jules said, tearing up again.

"He's wasting so much time going through pots and pans. Ridiculous." Traci said. "I'm sure that Carl guy had something to do with what happened to Chelsea. Burnhart? Is he related to the Burnhart family that owns the mattress company? That big warehouse over on the old toll bridge road?"

"Yeah." Jules nodded. "He's the only one in the family that still works there. He goes to school throughout the week and works there on weekends. And holidays, like today."

"So, he's there right now. Great! I'm going over there to talk to him. C'mon Jules." Traci lifted little Remy over her head, gave him a big kiss, and handed him to his father.

"For God's sake. It's Christmas Day, Tracinda." Randall tried to grab her arm, but she slipped away and was out the door with Jules right behind her.

"Don't worry. I'll go with them. It'll be okay. Try to relax."

"Yeah, right," Randall said and shook his head.

. . . .

MILO COULDN'T BELIEVE how many people would go to a mattress sale on Christmas Day. The Burnhart Mattress Warehouse was teeming with shoppers. He waved to Carlton, who was finishing up a sale and the three joined him at the rear of the store.

"Hi, Carl. How's business?" Traci asked and pressed down on a king-size mattress pad sample on the wall.

"Hi, fine. Do I know you?"

"No. But maybe you remember seeing me last night at Chelsea's party."

"I don't think so."

"Hey Carlton, how are you doing?" Jules intervened.

"I Ii Jules. Milo. I'm okay. Still can't believe the news about Chelsea, though. What brings you guys down here?" His face brightened a little.

"I saw you fighting with Chelsea. What was that about?" Traci continued.

"I don't know what you're talking about."

"Yes, sure you do. As a matter of fact, she caught you stealing something and was ready to throw you out. I think the police should know about that. Are you going to tell them? Or should I do it for you?"

"Okay, lower your voice. It was nothing." He motioned for them to be seated in a secluded corner. "I used to pocket some of her father's liquor. It was just my way of getting back at him."

"Yeah, I know he doesn't think any of us local guys are any good, especially for his daughter."

"What do you know about that, Milo?" Jules gave him a side-eye glance.

"Just his attitude. I've seen it before."

"Never mind that," Traci redirected. "Why were you crying? If it was nothing, like you said."

"I wanted to stay at the party. I needed to stay so I could spend some time with ... my friend. We hadn't seen each other in weeks. I just couldn't stand the idea of not being together on Christmas Eve, y'know?"

"You mean Chelsea, right?" Jules asked. It was obvious to everyone that it was not what he meant.

"Chris." He lowered his head then looked up at her.

"Chris?" Traci asked. "Chris who? The one with the red highlights and french manicure?

"No. The one with the mustache and red bottom sneakers."

"Oh," Jules and Milo exhaled and looked at each other.

"Who? Oh." Traci looked him over again. "Oh, gotcha."

"You're the one that rearranged the place cards." Jules whispered.

Carlton loosened his tie and gave her a little smile. "Chelsea and I were never ... we never. My parents thought Chelsea was the perfect girl for me. I couldn't tell them the truth. If you knew them, you'd understand. Anyway, Chelsea kept my secret to the end. God, I loved her for that. I'll always love her. I heard what happened between you two, Jules and that was just wrong.

She could be mean as a snake. I mean, everybody knew that about her, but she was good at keeping secrets. And trust me, the Parkers have plenty of secrets."

"So, your parents, they don't know?" Milo asked.

"They do now. I told them right after we got the news about Chelsea. I was pretty emotional. And very drunk, I'll admit. But I never thought that would be the last time I saw her."

"How did that go?" Milo pressed. "With your parents."

"Not great. I moved out. Didn't have a choice. Maybe it'll blow over. Maybe not. Either way, I'm glad I told them. After what happened to Chelsea, it was just too much to carry around. I'm sleeping in the back for now." The sad little smile flashed for a moment. "That's one perk of working in a mattress store."

"Speaking of that," Traci continued. "What happened to Chelsea?"

"I don't know. But, if anybody knows, I'll bet it's somebody in the family."

"Chelsea was an only child." Jules said puzzled.

"Right." Carlton acknowledged a customer waving to him near the twin mattress set display in the window.

"You're not saying her parents had something to do with it," Milo responded.

"You're right," Carlton said quickly. "I'm not saying it. Look, I've got to get back to work. Believe it or not, I have a sales quota. So, unless you want to take home one of our queen comfort coil spring mattress specials ..."

"No," Traci answered and turned away from him. Carlton accepted the dismissal and went to greet his customer. "I don't believe that guy," Traci whispered.

"I do," Jules said. "He's obviously in love with someone that he couldn't be with. He thought his parents would never accept him for who he really is. He was right. They threw him out. It's terrible. I feel bad for him. He was lonely and needed someone to talk to. I don't know why he picked Chelsea. But I guess love makes you do stupid things."

Milo didn't understand anything that was going on except that he could feel Jules pulling away from him. "Jules, listen ..."

Traci cut him off. "Well, fine. Go ahead and feel bad but if he's not the one that put Chelsea's lights out, then who else could it be? I don't believe for a minute she killed herself. Definitely not the type from what I could tell. And remember, it's your face on the video Jules."

"Right." Jules lowered her eyes. "I didn't like the part about them all having secrets. Like, what was he trying to say?"

"Or not say?" Milo watched Carlton put on a Santa Claus hat and pour on the charm with two more customers. "Look at him. I guess the show must go on."

Traci stood beside Milo and studied the scene. "There's got to be somebody Chelsea carried her secrets to, you know what I mean? Someone that she trusted."

Milo looked over at Jules who was deep in thought. "We need one of those 'well-known secrets' right now, huh?"

Traci turned to Jules. "Where did Chelsea get her hair and nails done?"

"Not one hundred percent sure. But my cousin Stella came by Chelsea's house before the party and did her nails and makeup. And mine. She closed her shop early just to take care of us like a personal glam squad. I think Chelsea was a regular client. Her shop is Estella's Nail Art on Rhodes Boulevard. If that helps."

Traci checked directions on her phone. "In the strip mall, right? I know that place."

"What did he mean about what happened between you and Chelsea?" Milo knew he should let it go but the question was just hanging in the air between them. "What exactly happened, Jules?"

"I was accepted into the apprenticeship program at Winchester School for the Arts. Remember that? It was supposed to help pay for grad school next year, plus it would be an awesome reference for my teaching career once I graduate."

Milo nodded and touched her arm gently. It was the one thing Jules had obsessed about for months. The pressure was incredible for her to get onboard at Winchester and he felt bad that he couldn't be more supportive, but he was overloaded with generating a profit through the catering business.

"It was important to me," Jules continued. "Well, Ms. Chelsea pulled some strings to get them to dump me and award it to her instead. It doesn't even matter that I have their acceptance in writing. The letter is worthless now ..." Jules looked up at him, "I don't know how I'm gonna pay for school. My parents will only help if I go out of state. And, you know what that means."

"I sure do." Milo knew it was their way of separating them and wasn't convinced that they didn't have a part in this sabotage with Winchester. But he would never say that out loud.

"The thing is, she didn't even need the money." Jules fought back her tears. "She didn't bother to submit a project according to the guidelines. So many of us put in the actual work. Not just me. It wasn't fair to anybody."

"Why didn't you tell me about this? You didn't tell me anything about this, Jules."

"Do you expect me to tell you everything, Milo?"

"Not everything. This. This you should have told me. And, that you went back after the party last night."

"If we head north," Traci interrupted, "Estella's place is just three streets over from here. Milo, go back and tell Randall we stopped for some 'girl time' at the nail salon. He'll understand." She pulled Jules by the elbow, and they rushed through the side exit, across the employee parking lot and out of sight.

• • • •

MILO PULLED INTO THE Parkers' driveway and parked his food truck along the hedgerow. There was only one thing that he understood. He had completed the job for Chelsea's party according to plan and he should get paid for the work. Period. He would express his condolences to the family and accept payment. It should only take a couple minutes. Then he could swing by Estella's and pick up Traci and Jules. He didn't want to face Randall without bringing them home with him.

He walked up to the front door and banged the iron knocker. Mrs. Parker opened the door and looked at him as if he was a total stranger.

"Why are you here?"

"Ma'am, I'm so sorry to hear about Chelsea. It's a shock for everyone."

"Ah, you want money, don't you?" Her eyes lowered as she slowly stepped back inside.

"Well, actually …" Milo paused and hoped that she would just follow through without further conversation.

"I'm sorry but this is not the time." She took one more step back and shut the door.

"Oh, this is exactly the time," he thought. The police had taken most of his stuff. Without the ability to purchase more supplies, he would never make it through the rest of his holiday season commitments. None of this was fair. He understood that the Parkers were grieving but what was he supposed to do? He walked back to his truck, took out his phone, and speed dialed the first number on his contact list.

"What's up? Where are you?" Randall answered.

"I'm at the Parkers."

"What are you doing there? Are Traci and Jules with you?"

"No, they're over on Rhodes getting their nails done. I'm trying to get paid."

"Trying?"

"Mrs. Parker slammed the door in my face."

"On my way."

• • • •

MILO WATCHED FROM THE driveway as Randall parked across the street and walked over to meet him. He was relieved to see Traci and Jules were in the car with him.

"Listen, angel," Randall said softly, "you can tell me all about what the nail lady said after I take care of this business with Milo. Okay? Stay in the car. We won't be long. Okay?" Traci rolled her eyes and finally nodded. Randall stepped out and slapped Milo on the arm. "Let's go."

At that same moment, Mr. Parker pulled into the driveway behind Milo's truck. They rushed up the path to the main entrance and met him at the door.

"Mr. Parker, we won't take up much of your time. I'm sure your wife mentioned the matter of payment for the birthday party catered by Milo and his team. We're here about that." Randall said with a steady gaze. Mr. Parker fished through his pocket and angled a key into the door lock.

"Yes, I'm sure she did. I don't carry my checkbook on me." He patted his pockets. "And we're just not accepting visitors at this time. You understand." He pushed the door open and stepped one foot inside. Randall placed his hand on the door and held it open.

"Of course not," he said coldly. "I'll wait right here to keep people away while you two go inside and take care of this issue with Milo. How's that?"

"Fine, fine. Come in."

The three men entered the house and found Mrs. Parker standing alone in front of the Christmas tree tossing presents into the fireplace, one by one.

"Oh, you're back," she said without turning around.

"I see you've lost your mind again," Mr. Parker said and brushed past her. "Where's your checkbook? Or have you burned that, too?"

"He's just angry. Tragedy brings out the worst in people, you understand." She took a sip from a frosted martini glass, glanced at Randall then looked back at her husband. "You said it should have been me."

"I did not," Mr. Parker snapped back.

"You're right. I said that I wished that it had been me instead of Chelsea. And you agreed with me."

Mr. Parker ripped the check out of the checkbook and handed it to Randall, then poured a drink from the bar. "It's just something that slipped out. Chelsea was my princess. What was I to say in that moment? Besides, this is not about you or me. It's about our daughter."

"Our daughter," Mrs. Parker murmured, then picked up another gift-wrapped box and tossed it into the flames. "Did I mention that the police are on their way? Oh look, here they are." She gave him a wry smile, shook the next gift box, and put it back under the tree.

Detective Gonzales and Officer Edmonds entered through the open front door. Traci and Jules slipped in behind them. Milo whispered to Randall, "What's going on?"

"No, you didn't. And you look like hell," Mr. Parker said and swallowed his liquor.

"I couldn't go back to sleep. The last place I saw Chelsea alive was in my bedroom."

"But she was found in the kitchen, ma'am," Gonzales interjected. His tone was gentle as he tried to engage the distressed woman.

"Yes, she went to the kitchen to make a cup of hot chocolate for me. That's where I found her, lying in the middle of the floor."

"Wait," Officer Edmonds spoke up. "Mr. Parker, you said that you had made a cup of hot chocolate for your wife and took it to her in the bedroom. Then you made one for yourself with the remainder of the milk and cleaned up the kitchen before you left for the night."

"Yes, that's exactly correct. I had an early flight out and decided to stay at the nearest hotel to beat the morning rush hour traffic. Of course, those plans fell through when I got the news about our daughter."

"Of course," Edmonds continued. "But why would your daughter need to make another cup? Seems odd."

"Plus, we already cleared out the kitchen and didn't leave anything to be cleaned. We left everything spotless," Jules chimed in. Randall patted her shoulder and placed his finger to his lips.

Officer Edmonds narrowed his eyes toward her. "But you said that you came back for a tray you left behind. If you had cleared everything, how is that true? Also, additional video footage shows you exited the house through the front door only carrying your purse. No tray." He pulled out a notebook. "But we'll get back to that."

"I had already stowed away the tray in the truck. That was my mistake for not telling her," Milo said. "If it has anything to do with the food, that's on me too. Jules didn't have anything to do with what happened to Chelsea."

Traci whispered to Randall, "What's he talking about?"

"Nothing." Randall mouthed 'be quiet' to Milo, then motioned to Officer Edmonds. "The second cup. Why?"

"Because my husband is an idiot or doesn't care, or both." Mrs. Parker glanced across the room in his direction. "I hate marshmallows."

"What?" Gonzales held up his hand. "What's that?"

"He put marshmallows in my hot chocolate. So, Chelsea offered to make another cup for me. She loved marshmallows, ever since she was a little girl, especially the homemade ones. She used to love them. God." She began sobbing.

"Homemade?" Officer Edmonds was unfazed by her tears.

"Yes, Milo made some," Jules answered.

"Is that right?" Edmonds jotted down a note.

"Yeah, I made a batch as a thank-you hostess gift for Chelsea," Milo offered. "People say they're really good."

"They are. Everybody loves them." Jules smiled at him.

"How many?" The officer paused his scribbling.

"It's just water, gelatin and sugar. The trick is to take your time, though," Milo said.

"Nobody cares." Randall nudged Milo and sighed. "Nobody cares about that part. Just answer the question."

"How many? A dozen. Twelve."

"How many did you put in the drink that you made for your wife, Mr. Parker?"

"I don't know. What difference does it make? Aren't we getting off the subject here?"

"Two," Mrs. Parker said with a hint of disdain. "Two floating in the cup, two more on the side in the saucer. Why?"

"There was a substance found in your daughter's system that may have contributed to her death. We're waiting on the final toxicology report to confirm what it is." Officer Edmonds kept writing. "In the meantime, we've got to account for everything she may have ingested during the last twenty-four hours of her life."

Mr. Parker pointed at Milo and erupted. "There you have it. Our daughter is gone, and it's his fault."

Randall leaned toward him and warned, "Hey, hold on. Don't get ahead of yourself, mister."

Traci whispered, "Randall, do something."

Randall took a deep breath. "Stay calm. Let's all stay calm. Alright?"

Mr. Parker called his bluff. "Stay calm? After what he put us through. I knew we should have never allowed these people to cater Chelsea's party. But she and her mother insisted. We could have hired Chef Palmer's team from Evan's Pier resort instead of this dog off the street."

"You wait a minute. Who do you think you are?" Traci pushed past Randall and lunged toward Mr. Parker. Randall wrapped his arms around her waist and pulled her back.

Milo asked Officer Edmonds, "What are you saying? What does that mean?"

Traci shouted, "They're saying the marshmallows you made were poison, and that's what killed Chelsea. That's what they're saying. You know what? You're all wrong and I can prove it. Where are the rest of the marshmallows? I'll eat them myself. All of them." Randall pulled her back again. "Where are they?"

Officer Edmonds went into the master bedroom and returned with the two marshmallows in a small plastic bag.

"Gonz? Are you counting?" Randall said. "What about the rest?"

"I know," Jules said softly. "I know where they are." She stepped forward and everyone followed her into the kitchen. "We put them in a small silver tin with the new logo on the side. MJ Catering."

"Our," Milo said. "Our new logo."

Traci whispered, "MJ Catering? When did that happen?"

"Later, angel." Randall patted her hand. "Edmonds, are you guys certain it was something she ate?"

"Obviously, it must have been the marshmallows," Mrs. Parker answered. "That was the last thing Chelsea had that night."

"And I drank the same cocoa mix with no marshmallows and I'm fine." Mr. Parker glared at Randall.

Jules opened the tin. There were only two marshmallows left inside.

Detective Gonzales asked Mr. Parker, "Where are the rest?"

"I have no idea. I don't keep an inventory of how many marshmallows are in this house. How insane is that question?"

"I took them," Jules said. "I put them in a little treat bag with some peppermint sticks for my cousin Estella's little ones. Her babies missed out because she worked Christmas Eve night to help us. And she doesn't make much even with tips. I didn't think Chelsea would miss any because... "

"Nobody cares about that part, Julie-girl," Randall said. "Just tell us how many you took."

"Six."

"Who is Stella?" Officer Edmonds turned to a new page in his notebook.

Randall answered. "Some fancy nail lady in the strip mall."

"She's a nail artist." Jules flashed her brightly polished fingertips at the officer. Traci showed off her nails, as well. "I would never give something to my family that could harm them. Never. Everyone is fine. I swear."

"Our. Our family," Milo said quietly.

Traci whispered to Randall, "What did he say? Our?"

"Shhh. Later, angel."

Fed up with the questioning, Traci reached for the tin, opened it, and started to grab a marshmallow. "Not poison."

Randall snatched the tin from her, closed the lid and handed it to Officer Edmonds. "Good God, Tracinda. This is evidence."

"Is everything alright?" Everyone's eyes turned to the tall thin man in a black wool turtleneck, jeans and red plaid house slippers standing in the doorway.

"Who are you?" Traci asked. Randall squeezed her hand. "Who is he?" she insisted.

"What are you doing here?" Mr. Parker demanded.

"I live here." The stranger walked calmly into the room.

"Sir?" Detective Gonzales stepped toward him.

"This is Les. Lester Daniels. He's my...," Mrs. Parker paused and let out a long sigh. "He's my friend."

"You sure don't waste any time, do you, Shanice?" Mr. Parker blurted out, his eyes still filled with rage.

"Chelsea is gone. What would be the point of continuing?" Mrs. Parker said, visibly exhausted. "Our marriage was over years ago. We were just waiting for Chelsea to graduate and head off to college before I filed for divorce. I didn't want her to have to go through a separation and custody battle. For the love of God, John just go away."

"Right." Mr. Parker straightened his shoulders. "Of course, right after Detective Gonzales makes the arrest. Clearly, we know what happened to our daughter." He glanced at Milo. "Go ahead and settle the matter so we can all get on with our lives. And Chelsea can rest in peace."

"No way!" Traci shouted. "There is no way that Milo had anything to do with what happened to Chelsea." She marched across the room to Officer Edmonds. "I'll prove it. Here, give me that." She snatched the plastic bag with the remaining two marshmallows and opened it. But right before she could reach inside, Mr. Parker grabbed her hand.

"No, stop. Don't do it." He squeezed her wrist until she winced in pain. "I'm sorry." He looked into her eyes and let go, then walked away from her with his palm pressed against his forehead, his pale face drawn and wearied.

Traci stared mercilessly at him and shouted at the man's back, "Tell them it wasn't Milo. Tell everybody how your princess was so broken up about the divorce that she couldn't sleep at night. She'd skip class and sit in her car and cry all day. She didn't want her real father to move in with them and take your place."

"I was her real father." Mr. Parker's voice cracked as he wiped his eyes.

"Lester is Chelsea's biological father." Mrs. Parker's voice was barely audible as she slumped against the wall.

Traci wasn't finished with the target of her wrath. She pointed at Mrs. Parker and blurted out, "And she wasn't going to give you a dime in spousal support. Once she cuts you off..."

"You said that you wished I had died instead of Chelsea. You wanted it to be me, John." Mrs. Parker said absently.

"Tracinda ... where'd you get all this from?" Randall asked.

Traci wiggled her brightly polished fingertips at him and mouthed the word 'Estella,' then faced John Parker again. "You're broke. Who's the dog in the street now, huh? Broke as a joke. Tell them! Nothing here belongs to you. Does it?"

Detective Gonzales approached Mrs. Parker and gently touched her arm. "Ma'am, I have to ask you and Mr. Parker to step into the other room with Officer Edmonds, please. You too, sir." He glanced at Lester Daniels and pointed to the hall leading to the great room. "We need to discuss a few details in light of this conversation."

The Parkers followed the officer through the heavy silence with Lester trailing behind them.

"Ms. Latimore, I'll have to check things out with your cousin regarding the half dozen marshmallows that you shared with them." Gonzales smiled at Jules once again. "In the meantime, you're free to go but..."

"I'll keep everyone close. No worries, Gonz," Randall interrupted and ushered everyone out of the patio door and along the path to the front yard. They looked back at the house and took in a breath of crisp winter air. Randall passed the check to Milo and patted him on the back. He placed his arm around Traci's shoulders and whispered as they continued down the path to the car, "Did you even consider the idea that Parker could have poisoned all the marshmallows?"

"Oh, babe. I wasn't really going to eat it. You worry too much."

"Let's get home before Brad and little Remy eat all the Christmas cookies. You riding with us, Jules?"

Milo was glad that Jules declined and would ride back with him. He stretched his arms above his head and took in a long deep breath, then lowered them around Jules and pulled her close. He showed her the amount on the check, and she squealed with delight. As they lingered next to the food truck, Detective Gonzales approached them.

"Oh, I see that you two are still here. Well, I might as well let you know this. John Parker just confessed to attempting to kill his wife and was placed under arrest. Mrs. Parker's personal physician is on his way to assist her. She's inconsolable. I suggest the two of you leave the property as soon as possible. You know how it goes. This place will be covered with news reporters in no time." He wished them well and disappeared toward the rear of the property.

"Can you believe that? If it had not been for you and your cousin, it might've been me getting locked up." Milo smiled at her.

"We'd have to break you out of there, for sure. But seriously, I think they were coming after me. My face on the video, remember?"

"If they'd put us in the same cell, it wouldn't have been so bad." He hugged her tightly. It felt wonderful to have her in his arms, but he had to ask. "Hey, why did you come back here after the party?"

"A stupid reason. Yeah, you were right. I was going to give Chelsea a piece of my mind. But I thought about how successful everything had been. It was a perfect party, and it meant so much for your business."

"Our business."

"Well, I didn't want to mess that up. So, after I got here, I just left."

"Out the front door."

"Yeah. And I took this." She opened her purse and showed him the sprig of mistletoe. "As a reminder. Stupid, right?"

"Listen..."

"No. Let me." She cleared her throat. "I know I've been acting..."

"Jealous?"

"Yes, jealous and it's not your fault. I guess I've been feeling scared."

"Well, sure. This whole thing has been crazy. It was enough to make anybody scared, even me."

"No, not that. I've been scared about us."

"What do you mean?"

"C'mon, Milo. I'm looking at starting grad school. And you'll be working night and day with catering gigs. New customers coming in every day."

"Pretty exciting, right?"

"And scary, Milo. What about us? What if there's no time for us anymore? Everything we're doing is pulling us apart. Don't you see that? I won't be able to be by your side once school starts up again. My schedule is so full and so is yours. I've been thinking, you need someone that can be..."

"You. I need you." He lifted the mistletoe over her head. "Do you remember the promise that I made to you that night?" He waited for her to return his smile and nod. "I still mean it. I don't know for sure how things will turn out with the business. Or how we'll pay for your classes. Right now, all I have for you is forever. Jules, that's my promise to you. Forever."

She kissed him and rested her head on his shoulder. "Merry Mistletoe, Milo."

"Marry me, my love." He held his breath until she whispered, "Of course, I will," and then his heart was free.

THE END

TRACE OF LACE

Traci pulled a Birston Bulletin from the purple and green campus news stand. "They found the body of the fourth girl."

"I heard that they found her near Grance Hall." Jules said and glanced over her shoulder. "They keep telling us to stay calm, but even with the new curfew, everybody's so scared right now. I'm glad I only have to come here for my job the rest of this week. Then, the big day." She took a deep breath and looked at Traci. "I don't know why I always start to cry when I think about my wedding. All my bridesmaids have gone. They moved out of the county to stay with relatives until all of this blows over. I can't blame them. But now it's just me and Milo. And that's okay. We'll be fine. I'm just nervous, I guess.

"Of course, but don't worry. It's going to be perfect." Traci said and ripped off the front page, folded it neatly and placed it in her handbag.

"Why do you want that?" Jules pointed at the paper.

"It has pictures of all the girls with their names and a little bit about their lives." Traci looked away. "I just wonder why they haven't caught the guy yet." She motioned for them to sit on a bench near the Administration building, then took out a packet of wet napkins and gave one to Jules. This section of the campus was typically bustling with students making their way to class or hanging out in the yard with friends. Today it was almost completely vacant.

"You're sure the killer is a man?" Jules said and rubbed the napkin across her fingers.

"It just feels like it to me." Traci tore open a small pouch of iced animal crackers and offered some to Jules.

"Hmm, I guess if you say so." Jules picked out a couple broken pieces and munched on them. "Can I tell you something that I haven't told anyone else?"

"Sure."

"I knew all of those girls."

"What?"

"Well, not really. I didn't know them like ... we weren't friends or anything. I don't mean that."

"Then what do you mean?" Traci balled up the empty pouch and stuffed it back into her bag.

"I mean, I tutored them. They were all psych majors and needed help to figure out a few things to finish up their requirements for graduation. You know?"

"No, I don't."

"Well, it was simple stuff, really. I'm sure that I wasn't the only person helping them. But still, it kinda freaks me out a little when I think about it."

"What did you help them do? Where were you? Was anyone else around? Anybody look, y'know ... suspicious?"

Jules laughed at the questions. "Suspicious? I don't think so. We met in all the regular places on campus. Nothing unusual. They brought some of their paperwork and I helped them fill out some forms. Trust me, there's always a ton of forms and applications to deal with. Nothing special. I don't know why I brought it up."

"Applications for what?" Traci said, then pulled out a pair of sunglasses, placed them on her face and tucked her hair behind her ears.

"Internships. You know what?"

"Tell me."

"All of them planned the same path. I guess that's not a big deal. Funny though, I just remembered that."

"Path? What do you mean?" Traci brushed the crumbs off her lap and stood up.

Jules followed her lead. "Oh, they planned the correctional facility internship path. Basically, you team up with a law enforcement team and help evaluate and collaborate on programs in a clinical setting."

"What does that mean? Evaluate. Who? Prisoners?" Traci adjusted her sunglasses and lifted her bag over her shoulder.

"Yeah, basically."

"Don't you think the police should know that part?"

"What part?"

"That you knew the girls and the rest of it."

"I think the police know what they're doing. They don't need me. Besides, I'm still trying to figure out if I want sherbet on the menu for my wedding reception. Milo wants to handle the food, but I told him that I would decide the menu. What was I thinking? I'm falling apart with everything. And I can't go back and tell him now at the last minute. Will you help me?"

"Sure." Traci smiled and gave Jules a quick hug. "But first, take me to where they found Celeste."

"You mean ..."

"The fourth girl."

· · · ·

JULES STOOD BACK ALONG the sidewalk and watched Traci step over the yellow police tape surrounding Grance Hall. She bit her lip as Traci took out her cellphone and started taking photos. Her heart skipped as a police officer appeared, confronted Traci and led her back to the sidewalk.

"I hope we're not in the way." Jules apologized.

Traci gave her a side-eye. "Of course, we're not in the way. How could we be in the way?"

"You're not in the way." The officer stepped closer to Jules and smiled. "Juliana Latimore, right?"

"How do you know me?"

"He's the cop they assigned to that Chelsea Parker situation, remember?" Traci said.

"Detective Gonzales."

"Oh, yes. I remember. That whole thing was so horrible I blotted it out of my mind." Jules managed a quick smile.

"That's understandable. So, what are you doing here? Are you a student?" He licked his lips and nodded.

Jules glance down at the Birston emblem on her sweatshirt. "Oh, no I'm not. I was. I graduated and work on campus now. Well, until after I get married. Then, I guess we'll have to figure out what's next after the wedding. What time is it? I can't be late for the final fitting with Markelle." Jules swiped her eyes to blot out the tears.

"Jules, there's nothing to worry about. You have plenty of time. Your dress is gorgeous. And Milo is a good guy, and everything will be fine."

Detective Gonzales lifted Jules' hand and admired her engagement ring. "Ah, well, I wish you the best. I'm sure you're going to be a beautiful bride. Milo? He's one of the cooks over at Moe's Tavern, right?" Jules pulled her hand away and looked at Traci.

Traci moved between them. "He's the owner of MJ Catering. But you knew that, Detective Gonzales."

"Right. You didn't tell me why you're here." He looked past her, his gaze remained on Jules.

"Just curious." Traci stared at him, trying not to be triggered by his arrogance.

"About?"

"Why you haven't caught the Campus Killer. I assume that's why you're here. Am I right?"

"Hmm, the 'Campus Killer'. Don't let the headlines scare you." Detective Gonzales said.

Jules lowered her voice. "Plenty of reasons to be scared. I've got to walk this campus every day. Makes you look over your shoulder all the time, that's for sure."

"No need for that. I'm happy to escort you wherever you need to go." He stepped along the opposite side of Jules.

"Well, I need to get to Markelle's for my appointment. I don't want to be late."

"I'll walk with you, Jules. It's not far from here." Traci said.

"No need for that either." Detective Gonzales reached out again. "I'm headed in that direction next. And, I have my private vehicle today. I can get you to your appointment on time. So, what do you say?" He grasped her elbow and gently pulled her forward. Jules shrugged toward Traci and walked alongside of him.

Traci called out to her. "Tell him about the interns."

"The what?" He said without glancing back at her and continued leading Jules across the grassy knoll toward the parking lot.

"Jules knew those girls. She helped get the interns' applications done to work with the prisons. Don't you think you should write this down?"

"No need."

. . . .

MILO GAVE LITTLE REMY a high five as Randall kneeled beside him and tied his shoelaces.

"This kid can never keep his shoes on. Gets it from his mother. Drives me crazy." Randall lifted his son onto the walnut Cambridge style bench along the back wall of Griffin and Sons Tailor Shop and handed him a small bag of fruit snacks. He glanced over his shoulder to Milo, who was positioned in front of the floor-length mirror. "I'm gonna apologize in advance for any mishaps with your ring bearer. Traci's been practicing with him all week, but I make no promises."

"Hey, don't worry about it. That's the least of our problems right now." Milo wiped the perspiration from his brow as the tailor and his assistant orbited around him. He finished buttoning the crisp white dress shirt while the assistant wrapped the cummerbund around his waist and snapped it into place. Mr. Griffin, the shop owner, lifted the tuxedo jacket over his arms, tugged at the shoulders and whispered, "Perfect, perfect."

Milo took a deep breath and stepped back to get a full view of the outcome. "I think I clean up pretty good. Maybe Mr. Latimore will finally approve of me."

"Her old man still giving you a hard time?" Randall took his jacket from the assistant and waved him off. He slipped it on and smoothed the sleeves across his arms. He refused the cummerbund with a scowl.

"We're still not sure he's coming to the wedding. It's got Jules on edge." Milo studied the shoe selection lined up in front of him and decided on the smooth black leather loafer with a steel gray tassel. He tried them on and took another glance in the mirror, then decided on the pair without the tassel.

"He'll come around. Don't sweat it. Just keep your head up and stay on your grind. You've come a long way. Jules is a sweet girl. You did good." Randall flexed his arms, buttoned the jacket, then loosened it again.

"Yeah, I can't believe she agreed to marry me." Milo smiled and offered his wrist to the assistant to add the cufflinks. "Hey Randall, I never thanked you for everything you've done for me. Not just the wedding stuff. Everything."

"It's all good." Randall moved over to the mirror and checked his reflection with a frown. "You look okay, but I look like a pit bull in a tiara. Guess there's nothing Traci can do about that. She swore to me that she's not going to cry at your wedding. She owes me a steak dinner if she does. I think that's a safe bet." He licked his lips and laughed. "Bless her little vegan heart."

Milo stood next to him and grinned. "No, seriously. When you guys got married, I thought she was going to just ... throw me away. You know what I mean?"

"Yeah, I get it. You were a kid. What else would you expect? But, I knew from the start you two were a package deal. There's no way Traci will ever let go of you. Now she's got Jules as a bonus. So, like I said, it's all good." He rubbed his palms together and stepped away. "Listen, I'm gonna have to wrap this up and go take care of something."

"Something I can help with?"

"Naw. I've gotta drop one of my part-time security guards off the roster and find a replacement, ASAP. And that ain't gonna be easy."

"Wow, what happened?"

"KMP has put all available officers on the campus homicide cases. So, the guys are getting all the overtime they can over there. That means I'm short staffed without those part-timers. Then this last guy, Gonzales, just got put on administrative leave pending a psych eval." He dropped the dress slacks on the floor and pulled on his jeans. "Dude mishandled a hostage situation, and everything went south. Messed his head up. I can't put him on assignment at a client's site. You never know when somebody's gonna snap."

"I remember that. The hostage was a nanny and a little girl, right? The fiancé killed them both. Everybody's still talking about that. Did they ever catch the guy?"

"Yeah, that's the one. No, they didn't. Not sure if it's related to what's been happening near the college or not. Traci's been obsessed with all of it. She doesn't think KMP is working hard enough. It's a full time job for me to keep her from sticking her nose in it."

Randall snatched his cellphone away from little Remy. "How'd you get this? Are you some kind of pickpocket? I swear, you gotta watch him every second." He peeled off the tuxedo jacket and said, "Too tight." Then tossed it at Mr. Griffin, who sucked his tongue, pulled the sleeves right-side out, flapped the garment back into shape and handed it off to the assistant. Randall ignored the man's glare and checked the notifications on his phone.

"Surely you won't be wearing that at the wedding, sir." Mr. Griffin said and pointed to the gun holstered across Randall's abdomen.

"Is that right? Who's gonna take it from me?" Randall said with a tone that blocked any attempt at a response from the man who turned around and motioned for his assistant to meet him in the backroom. "They just put Birston on lock-down. They found a suspicious package near one of the dorms. Probably nothing."

"What?" Milo spun around and pushed past the others. "I've got the find Jules."

"Calm down, cowboy." Randall placed his hand on Milo's shoulder and looked him in the eye. "Traci is with her. They're picking out flowers, or earrings, or cupcakes. I don't know."

"Okay, alright." Milo said and returned to the mirror. "Besides, I'm going to meet her later for dinner."

Remy waved goodbye as his father guided him toward the front door of the shop.

"Trust me, wherever they are, Traci's not going to let Jules out of her sight."

. . . .

DETECTIVE GONZALES accepted another glass of wine from Markelle and settled down in the loveseat near the dressing room. He surveyed the racks filled with satin and tulle dresses, took a sip, and nodded at Jules. "So, on the way over, you were saying your father is very 'picky' about everything."

"Yeah, he's not crazy about this wedding." Jules drained her glass. Markelle refilled it immediately.

"The wedding? Or the groom?"

"Both, I guess. Yeah, both."

"But you're not letting that stop you, apparently."

"Why should I?"

"I don't know, but maybe your father does."

"Knows what?"

The detective placed his glass down and shrugged, then leaned in closer to her.

Jules studied the paisley printed carpet between their feet. "Never mind. I shouldn't bother you with all my family drama. But sometimes I feel like my head is going to explode if I don't talk about it."

"Why don't you talk to your girlfriend about it?"

"Who?"

"The one that likes to take pictures of crime scenes."

"Traci? She's more like a sister. Well, I mean like a sister to Milo, but not me. She cares about me and everything, I think. It's a long story, how they met and all that."

"I'm familiar with it."

"Oh sure, you know her husband Randall from when he was a cop, too. I guess you know pretty much everything about everybody here. That's how it is in a small town like Keeferton." She laughed and lowered her voice. "Thanks for listening, anyway. And, for the ride over."

"Do you need a ride home?"

"I'm going to meet Milo at Sabastian's for dinner. It's right across the street." She looked out the window and pointed to the crowd of diners under the bistro's blue striped awning. "He should be here in about thirty minutes."

"Then, I better get moving. If you need any extra security for the wedding, let me know."

"I think Randall has got that covered. Thanks, though. But you're welcome to come to the wedding if you like. I don't have any more invitations, but I can add you, and a plus one."

"Are you sure?"

"I'm sure." She retrieved her planner and pen from her bag. "Chicken or fish?"

"Fish."

"For both?"

"Both?"

"You and your guest. Girlfriend, maybe?"

"Oh, yeah. Both."

"Got it," Jules said and tore off a piece of note paper. "Here's the address. This Saturday morning at nine-thirty. I know it's short notice. Milo's going to kill me if I keep adding people to the guest list."

"No one is going to kill you." He accepted the note and let his touch linger against her palm.

"What is your friend's name? I'll add it to the list."

"Oh, wait. You know what? I could use a favor if you don't mind." The detective stood and stashed the note in his shirt pocket.

"What?"

"I'd like to buy something for my friend to wear. Like you said, it is short notice. I know how you women can never decide what to wear. Am I right?"

"Ha! I totally understand. And it's hard to find something at the last minute. What do you need from me?" Jules tucked away her planner and stood up.

"Can you try on a few dresses for me and give me your opinion? She's about your same size. How about this one?" He pointed out a sheath dress beautifully styled on the mannequin.

"Sure, I can do that. I've tried on a million dresses already. What's a few more?" She laughed and waved to Markelle, who undressed the mannequin and followed Jules to the fitting room.

When she emerged, the detective placed his hand over his heart. "Fabulous."

"And it's almost a perfect fit." Jules spun around. "You should get a little coverup, just in case. Like this one." As she reached for the garment, her phone chimed her favorite ringtone. She scrambled over to answer and accept the video. Milo's smiling face greeted her.

"I'm at Sabastian's. Where are you?"

"Oh no, I'm still at the bridal shop. I thought you were going to meet me here first. No problem, I'm on my way."

"Hey, wear that dress for dinner. You look amazing!"

"Nope, you wouldn't like it so much if you saw the price tag."

"Okay, I'll just take a screenshot then. That's all I can afford right now."

Jules laughed and ended the call, then turned back to Detective Gonzales.

"I got things mixed up. I've got to go. I hope you pick this one. I think it's the prettiest one in the shop." She rushed back to the fitting room, then spun around and faced him again. "Oh, I should give you my work schedule so you can meet me there. At least until they find the Campus Killer and lock him up."

"No need. I know how to find you."

Markelle held open the fitting room door and Jules stepped back inside.

Detective Gonzales motioned for her to join him. "I need you to deliver that dress to me in a gift box. Here's my card. I expect you to be discreet. Use an unbranded vehicle. Understood?"

• • • •

A COLORFUL PATCHWORK of shadows flickered across the bare wooden floor of the Myer Chapel sitting room. The door creaked open slowly. Mrs. Latimore peaked around and announced herself.

"Juliana, it's Mommy. Are you decent?"

Traci pulled the door open wide and Jules stepped forward like a glamorous centerpiece. The train of her veil draped around her feet and the intricate beaded details of her wedding dress sparkled in celebration of this greeting. Overwhelmed, the bride held out her arms and began to weep. "Mommy, I'm so glad you're here."

"Nope, nope. No tears. Not now. We just got your makeup set, Jules." Traci patted a small cotton pad across her cheeks and shook her finger under Jules' nose.

"I'm speechless," Mrs. Latimore said as she clasped her daughter's hands. "Absolutely, stunning." She turned away, unzipped her purse, and rummaged through its contents until she found a small manilla envelope. She pulled back the flap slowly and lifted out a small strip of Chantilly lace. "Here, sweetheart. I want you to have this. It's from my veil that I wore on my wedding day. I pray it brings you good luck for your future with Milo."

"You and daddy have been married thirty-two years. I think that's the kind of luck I need." Jules took the lace and held it to her chest. "Thank you so much."

"I don't mean to be rude, but it's almost time." Traci said and fluffed up the tiny pale blue rosebud petals in her wrist corsage that matched her satin maxi-dress with flutter sleeves.

Mrs. Latimore nodded, blew her daughter a kiss and stepped toward the door. "Oh, one more thing. I convinced your hard-headed father to be here and walk you down the aisle. He's running late, but he's on his way."

"What?" Jules said, her face beaming with joy. "How did you convince him?"

"After thirty-two years, I know how to get what I want." Mrs. Latimore chuckled and closed the door behind her.

Jules spun around and grabbed Traci by the shoulders. "Can you believe it? After all that stonewalling, he's finally going to give me his blessing. I know it probably sounds silly, but it really means a lot to me!"

Traci smiled and loosened herself from her grip. "I understand. If it's important to you, then it's important to me, too. I'm glad it's working out, Jules. Honestly, I'm really happy for you."

"I wonder if Markelle can sew this into my dress." She draped the piece of lace across her sleeve. "I'm going to call her and ask."

"Jules, it's too late for that. We've got to get everybody in place in twenty minutes. Milo has been pacing around the courtyard since dawn." Traci laughed and placed her fingertips on Jules' cheek. "There's no time for this now."

"Well, okay. But will you run and tell the others that my daddy is coming, and we might have a late start?"

"Sure, I can do that." Traci stepped back and smiled at the young bride. "You look beautiful, Jules. Everything is going to be perfect," she said and left the room.

As soon as Traci was gone, Jules closed the door and rushed over to the corner of the room. She grabbed her phone from her bag and tapped Speed Dial 8.

"Hi, Markelle, this is Juliana Latimore. Thank you, thank you. Yes, I'm so excited. The dress is unbelievable. I absolutely love it." She lowered her voice to a whisper. "Can you do a quick little modification? It's a simple stitch on, like a patch. You can do it by hand. It's no big deal, right?"

• • • •

TRACI SPOTTED MILO and Randall standing together under the floral arch suspended around the garden gate entrance of the chapel. Randall waved to her, shrugged, and pointed to their son, who was swatting him on the butt with the white satin ring bearer's pillow.

"Randall, seriously." Traci pulled little Remy to her side. "Anyway, Mr. Latimore is coming, and Jules is over the moon."

"Wow, that's something I never expected to hear," Milo said, wide-eyed and grinning.

"That's a good sign, I guess." Randall slapped him on the back.

"Yeah, but that means the ceremony is going to start later than planned." Traci took the pillow from little Remy and checked it for stains.

"It'll be worth it. Jules deserves the best." Milo reached into his pocket and pulled out his cellphone. "I've gotta talk to her."

"Milo, no. That's bad luck." Traci reached for his phone, but he dodged her hand.

"I won't do video, okay?" Milo pressed the phone to his ear.

Randall smiled and wrapped his arm around Traci's waist. "Relax." He gave her a quick kiss on the cheek. "You look gorgeous, by the way." She stopped resisting and rested against his shoulder. They both took a deep breath.

"She's not answering. I don't like that." Milo looked at Traci. "You try."

"I will not." Traci gave Milo a side-eye.

Randall squeezed her waist against him. "Do it, angel."

"Okay, okay." Traci frowned and pulled out her phone that was tucked in her waistband. She called Jules' number, then frowned. She tried again, with no success. "That's weird. I'll go back upstairs and check on her, just in case."

"I'm coming with you," Milo said, and glanced at Randall for support.

"Come on, let's go." Randall considered how to appease Traci's red face and pursed lips. "It's okay, we'll talk to her through the keyhole. Lighten up. It's only the most important day in Milo's life." The more Traci rolled her eyes, the more he laughed.

Traci acquiesced and let the two follow her to visit with Jules before the ceremony. She deposited Remy on his uncle Brad's lap along the way. The three mounted the narrow staircase in the rear of the entrance hall to the improvised dressing room on the second level.

"Jules don't open the door. Milo is with me." Traci called out as they reached the top of the stairs. She knocked twice, pushed the door slightly ajar, and slipped through. "Jules?"

Randall slapped Milo on the back. "Traci's just as nervous as the two of you. It's just a matter of time before she's in a puddle of tears." Milo chuckled and wiped his sweating palms against his pant leg. The door banged open and startled the men back on their heels.

"She's gone." Traci stood before them, pointing to the empty room.

"What do you mean?" Milo said, stepping inside and looking around. "I don't understand." He tried calling her again. "Still no answer."

"Alright, alright." Randall held up his hand. "Let's think everybody. Traci, what were you talking about the last time you were with her?"

"She asked me to let everyone know that we were starting late." She paced around the room. "Her bag is missing. I don't like this, Randall. I got a funny feeling."

"Why would she take her bag? Where would she go?" Milo wiped his face and loosened his collar.

"Wait," Traci brightened up. "Maybe she went to see Markelle at the bridal shop."

"Why in the world would she go there now?"

"She wanted to have something sewn onto her dress ..."

"What? That makes no sense." Milo said. "I don't understand. Our wedding is supposed to start in a few minutes. What is she thinking?"

Randall placed his hand on Milo's shoulder, "Hey, listen. Here's some advice. You will never understand how your wife thinks. Get used to it."

"That's not funny, Randall." Traci said and folded her arms.

Randall chuckled and directed the other two ahead of him out of the room and back down the stairs. "Everything's going to be okay. Let's take a look outside."

Traci rushed ahead of them and stood in the spot where Jules' car should have been parked. She noticed something in the gravel, reached down and picked it up. "Oh no, babe."

"What's happening?" Randall stepped up to examine the item. "What's that?"

"It's the lace from her mother's veil." Traci said and turned to her husband, her voice trembling. "I don't like it. Something's wrong."

"What's that doing here?" Milo said.

"This is what she wanted Markelle to add to her dress." Traci's eyes welled over with tears.

"She probably dropped it by accident when she got in the car. Don't get worked up about it." Randall took Traci's face in his hands and waited for her to regain her composure. "Alright? We'll just go over there and retrieve Milo's bride. Case closed."

They walked over to Milo's car and interrupted the kids decorating it with streamers

"I'll drive, M." Randall said. Milo tossed him the keys, helped Traci into the backseat and climbed into the passenger's side. Randall started up the Impala and peeled out across the front lawn onto Myer Boulevard toward downtown Keeferton.

· · · ·

"SORRY. WE'RE CLOSING early. One of our clients is getting married today, and she was nice enough to invite me." Markelle smiled as she attempted to lock the door of the bridal shop.

"We're looking for Jules Latimore." Milo brushed past her and entered the dark room. The others followed him inside. Milo showed her the screenshot he had taken during the video call he had with Jules. It was his most recent picture of her, and she had been in the bridal shop that day.

"Yes, that's her." Markelle nodded and smiled. She flipped on the showroom lights and dropped her keys on the counter.

"Her car is parked out front. We thought she was in here." Randall said.

"Well, she did call about a last-minute alteration ..."

"About this?" Traci held up the strip of lace.

"Yes, but when she didn't show up, I assumed that she changed her mind. It's typical for brides to be a little anxious on their big day. One lady wanted me to remove the train from her dress five minutes before walking down the aisle. The entire train. Can you believe that?"

Traci took Milo's phone and looked at the photo. "That's the wrong dress."

"What do you mean?" Milo squinted and then enlarged the picture.

"I was with her when she picked out her wedding dress. That's not it." Traci glanced at Randall.

Markelle looked at it again. "That's true. She selected the most beautiful BellaModa dress with the cascading ..."

"Maybe she was checking out other options. Probably tried on every dress in this place." Randall said.

"Not quite." Markelle laughed. "She did try on a few extra ones for her friend, though. He selected that one she's wearing in the picture and wanted it delivered to him, but he showed up today and picked it up instead."

"Friend? What friend?" Milo said and looked at Traci who shrugged. He stepped closer to Markelle and towered over her, gripping his phone in his fist.

Traci moved away toward the sales counter. "What's the name of the dress Jules is wearing in that picture?"

"CeraFina Royale. Gorgeous dress." Markelle said avoiding eye contact with Milo. "I could check the sales ledger but I'm certain that was it."

"Who cares about that?" Milo's voice exploded.

Randall pressed his arm against Milo's chest and turned to Markelle. "Who was with her that day?"

Markelle darted away from the men toward the door. "Oh, I think I should let you talk to the owner. I just work here. I'm really not supposed to discuss any of our clients' business with ...

"What do you mean? It's a simple question." Milo followed her across the room.

"I can't." Markelle opened the door. "They could fire me. I can't lose my job. You understand, right?"

Randall pulled Milo back and patted his shoulder. "This is Ms. Latimore's fiancée. She just disappeared from the chapel on their wedding day. We're trying to find out where she went. That's all. Can you tell us who she was with when you last saw her?"

"Maybe she got cold feet. It happens."

"Just answer the question." Randall took a deep breath, then took a step forward.

"I'll just say that he was a police officer. That should ease your minds."

"A cop? Why would Jules ..." Milo shook his head.

"Milo, what day did you take that picture?" Traci said.

"Thursday. Why?"

"Oh! Sure, that makes sense. I met Jules on campus that day. I asked her to show me where they found Celeste and there was a cop with us.

Milo and Randall spun around and stared at Traci. "Who is Celeste?"

"The fourth girl. The Campus Killer."

Randall grasped his forehead. "Why were you ... what were you even doing around ... Tracinda, why?"

"Do you have to talk about that part right now?" Milo said.

"Right. It was nothing." Traci said. "We were there, and I guess we sorta bumped into that officer and started talking. He gave her a ride for her last fitting on Thursday. And he's been escorting her around campus for the last couple of days so that she'd feel safe. You know, because of the Campus Killer still being loose and ..."

"Wait. What?" Milo said. "Jules never told me anything about needing a police escort."

"She didn't want to worry you. Anyway, at least we know ..."

"We know what?" Randall said. "That you were digging around a crime scene at Birston College? Tracinda, how many times do I have to tell you not to get involved in active investigations? This snooping around is going to get you in trouble one day. The kind of trouble that I can't get you out of."

"Randall," Milo said. "Man, this is not the time for you two to go off. Seriously."

"You're right." Randall nodded at Milo and then approached his wife. "Angel, what's the name of the officer you met?"

"I'm not sure." Traci whispered. "You know I'm not good at remembering names."

"I know but this is important. So, focus and try really hard to remember this one."

"Garcia."

Randall reached for his phone. "Okay, I'll call over to KMP Dispatch and see if I can get any information about this."

"If she's with him, then I know she's safe. But why doesn't she answer her phone?" Milo said.

Traci snapped her fingers. "Oh wait. No, not Garcia. Gonzales. Detective Gonzales."

"Why does that name sound familiar?" Milo said.

"Chelsea Parker's murder." Traci answered.

"Oh, God. Yeah, I remember him."

Randall lowered his phone. "Tracinda, are you sure? Are you *absolutely* sure?

"Yeah. I'm positive. Go ahead and call them."

"Romeo Gonzales is no longer in uniform with KMP. He was removed from duty because of ..." Randall walked over to the shop keeper and pointed his finger at her. "Listen, Markelle, you need to understand that if Jules is with him, she could be in danger."

"Is that the guy you told me about at Griffins?" Milo said.

"Same one," Randall said without lifting his gaze from the target of his interrogation.

Milo grabbed Markelle by the arm and pulled her around to face him. "Where did he take her? Tell me."

"I don't know anything. And I can't tell you anything."

"Which is it? You don't know or you can't tell me?" Milo said and jerked her forward again.

Randall separated them and motioned for Milo to calm down. Then he came back to Markelle who was rubbing her arm and forcing back tears. "Let's start with this, what address did he give you to deliver the dress?"

"Got it," Traci shouted from the sales counter and ripped out a page from the ledger. "CeraFina Royale, size 12, turquois blue. Sold: Romeo Gonzales, 1468 Lotus Ct, West Keeferton. Let's go!"

The three race out of the store and Markelle locked the door behind them.

• • • •

RANDALL DROPPED THE gear shift into neutral, coasted the car down the service road behind the West Keeferton subdivision and parked behind a community dumpster.

"Okay, I'm going up there," Randall pointed to the small rustic cottage at the end of the lane. "I can see a car parked along those bushes so he's probably inside. He's armed, no doubt about it, but he knows me. So, I might be able to get inside. The main thing is to keep him cool until KMP gets here." He turned around to face Traci in the backseat. "You stay here with Milo. No matter what happens, stay in the car. Tracinda, are you listening to me?"

Milo opened the glove box, pulled out a Glock 19, checked the clip and tucked it in his cummerbund, then jumped out the passenger side and started up the lane to the cottage.

"What the ..." Randall said and raced up to match his stride. "When did you get that?"

"When things started popping off at Birston," Milo said. "What did you expect?"

"That's fair," Randall said with a smirk. "But slow down and let me handle this." He turned back and pointed at Traci watching from the backseat window, and mouthed, "Stay there."

They reached the cottage just as Detective Gonzales emerged from beside his car. He was carrying a large box with the embossed chartreuse and pink bridal shop logo.

"Hey Gonz, how's it going?" Randall said with a casual smile.

"Randall, what are you doing here?"

"Thought I'd stop by and talk to you about some assignments I have coming up. A few new clients you might be interested in working with." Randall searched the man's expression. "What's in the box?"

"Where is she?" Milo said.

"Who is she?" Gonzales tensed up and dropped the box on the hood of his car. "And who are you to be asking questions?"

"Listen, don't worry about him," Randall said and waved it off.

"What's this about?" The man's jaw tightened, and eyes narrowed.

"You know who I'm talking about." Milo took a step forward, and the detective did the same.

"Guys, settle down. Let's go inside and talk. I do have a couple of things I'd like to ask you, Gonz." Randall said, still smiling.

"You both need to get out of here."

The standoff was interrupted by the sound of broken glass and Traci shouting from the inside of the cottage.

"She's here. I found her!"

Randall pulled his weapon before Gonzales had a chance to react. "Hands on your head. Do it." Then, he nodded toward Milo, "Go, man!"

Milo leaped onto the porch, kicked the front door open and ran through the cottage checking every room. He found Jules seated in the master bedroom with her mouth taped shut. Her arms and ankles were strapped to the chair. Traci was kneeling next to her trying to peel away the tape.

Milo pushed Traci aside and finished the job.

"Oh my God, Milo. I can't believe you found me. I can't believe it."

"Are you okay?" Milo wiped her tears and kissed her.

"I'm okay." Jules said and twisted her wrists trying to get free.

Traci reached in her waistband and drew out a switchblade, opened it, and looked up at Milo. "Don't tell Randall about this."

"No problem," Milo said and watched Traci make quick work of cutting through the bands. As soon as her arms were free, Jules wrapped them around his neck. "Did he *touch* you?" he whispered.

"No." Jules said and gave him a little smile.

Traci looked out of the broken window and caught a glimpse of two KMP squad cars approaching the property. She surveyed the room and noticed newspaper clippings scattered across the bed and leaned in to take a closer look. She recognized one of the faces.

"Celeste," Traci said and then studied the others. "These are all engagement photos from the Times Daily." She walked back to Jules who was standing in a full embrace with Milo. "These are the girls from Birston. He took them, too. Didn't he?"

"Yes," Jules whispered. "He did." She sat back down and buried her face in her hands.

"Police," the KMP officer announced himself, entered the room and walked directly up to Jules. "Are you alright, Miss?"

"I'm alright. He didn't hurt me. He just kept talking about his last case and running through different scenarios over and over again. Then, he'd ask me what I thought about it."

"Why?" Traci said.

"He was trying to figure out what went wrong. He thought with my training, that I could help him do that."

"The help he needs, I got." Milo said and stormed out of the room. He pushed past the officers standing with Randall, grabbed Gonzales by the shoulder, spun him around and pounded his fist into the man's jaw. He stood over him and shouted, "Get up."

Randall pulled Milo back and bumped his chest. "Think, man. Think." He looked back over his shoulder at the arresting officer and said, "You didn't see that."

The officer glanced at his colleague and pointed at Gonzales. "Get him up and cuff him."

Jules stepped outside and Milo swept her up in his arms again. "I thought that I had lost you. I don't know what I would do if that happened."

Randall helped Traci down the stairs to join them. He brushed her hair back and sighed. "You know what I always say. 'One day you're going to listen to me, but ...'"

"I know, I know. 'But today is not that day.'" Traci chimed in.

"Seriously." He pulled her close and kissed her forehead. "Did you get hurt?"

"No," Traci brushed off her hands. "Well, I ripped my dress. See here." She showed him where the seam on the side of her dress had split to the top of her thigh.

"Oh, I like it." Randall smirked and slid his hand along the curve of her hip. "Sexy." Traci blushed and pushed him away.

Milo's cellphone rang. He looked at the screen with a grin, accepted the call, and passed it to Jules.

"Juliana Marie, I've called you five times, and you don't answer. What's going on?"

"Mommy! Oh, there was a ... problem but everything is okay now. I'm fine. Everything's fine."

"Stop it. Stop it, Carl. Give me that."

"Mommy! What's wrong? What's happening?"

"Hello? How does this work?"

"*Daddy!*"

"Yes, it's me. It's me. Oh, I see you now. Oh my, you look so beautiful, my little lamb. Just like your mother. Well, I'm here at the church. Tell me what you want me to do."

"Just wait there. I'm on my way!" Jules ended the call and started sobbing.

"Oh, let me fix your makeup." Traci rushed over, turned the inside of her cuff to dab and blot under each eye. Then she pulled the piece of Chantilly lace from around her wrist corsage. "I found it." She took down one of the curls in Jules' hair and braided in the piece of lace then wrapped it around the base of her bun like a halo and pinned it in place. "There, that'll do."

"Thank you. You're the best, Traci," Jules said and looked into Milo's eyes. "Do you like my dress?"

"I love it," Milo said. "I think we're ready, don't you?"

"Hold up," Randall said. "You mean to tell me after all we've just been through you want to go back to the ceremony like nothing happened?"

"Yes," the three shouted in unison and headed down the path to the car.

Randall turned to the arresting officer and shrugged.

"It's alright, go ahead. We've gotta go through the place. We're going to be here for a while. We can get a statement from each of you later."

"C'mon Randall," Traci shouted from the car window. "Let's go!"

    • • • •

TRACI AND RANDALL TOOK their seats just in time to watch Mr. Latimore accompany his daughter down the aisle. Traci took a deep inhale to the count of ten and glanced back at Randall. "I'm not going to cry."

"Bet," Randall chuckled and gave Milo a thumbs-up who was waiting impatiently at the altar.

As Mr. Latimore released her hand, Milo stepped up, wrapped his arms around Jules and gave her a long, sumptuous kiss. The guests roared with laughter and applause.

"It looks like Milo decided it's best to start with dessert first." Reverend Delano chuckled. "Let's continue with the nuptials. I know it's only a formality, but it's why we're all here, right? Everyone in place, please."

Little Remy handled his ring bearer duties like a champ. Randall waved him over to join his parents and gave him a high-five. Traci wrangled him past the other guests on their row, retrieved the bow tie from his clinched fist and clipped it back on his collar. He settled onto her lap and rested his cheek against her neck.

"Are you crying, yet?" Randall whispered.

"No, I'm fine." Traci hugged their son and continued watching the couple exchange vows.

"You're about to start." Randall said. "I can tell. And remember, I take my steak rare and don't forget my favorite sauce from Moe's."

"I'm not going to. I'm perfectly fine with this. Milo is a grown man now. I know it was hard for me to accept it, but ..."

"Right. You two have been side-by-side since he was fourteen and you found him working as a field hand at Bent Willow Farm. You've been through some tough times together. Things could have gone the worst way for his life, but you kept after him. And look at where he is today. That's all you, angel. You should be proud of yourself and Milo."

"And Jules is a wonderful girl. They're very happy together. And I'm happy for them." Traci sniffled and busied herself tying little Remy's shoe laces.

"After all that, you're telling me you've got no tears."

"Well ... no." Traci looked back up as the minister pronounced them "man and wife."

"You may kiss your bride, again." Reverend Delano made room for them, and the crowd applauded and snapped pictures.

"You know," Randall slipped his arm around Traci's shoulder. "One day that's going to be little Remy."

Traci started crying, her wail echoed through the chapel hall as Milo and Jules waved to her, then walked hand-in-hand down the aisle and out of sight. Randall gently pulled Traci's head against his shoulder and whispered. "Gotcha."

THE END